Phoebe
the Fashion
Fairy

To Charlotte Ingle,
a real fashion fairy, with love

Special thanks to
Sue Mongredien

If you purchased this book without a cover, you should be aware
that this book is stolen property. It was reported as "unsold and
destroyed" to the publisher, and neither the author nor the publisher
has received any payment for this "stripped book."

No part of this work may be reproduced, stored in a retrieval
system, or transmitted in any form or by any means, electronic,
mechanical, photocopying, recording, or otherwise, without written
permission of the publisher. For information regarding permission,
write to Rainbow Magic Limited c/o HIT Entertainment,
830 South Greenville Avenue, Allen, TX 75002-3320.

ISBN 978-0-545-22173-3

Text copyright © 2005 by Rainbow Magic Limited.
Illustrations copyright © 2005 by Georgie Ripper.

All rights reserved. Published by Scholastic Inc., 557 Broadway,
New York, NY 10012, by arrangement with
Rainbow Magic Limited.

SCHOLASTIC, LITTLE APPLE, and associated logos are
trademarks and/or registered trademarks of Scholastic Inc.
RAINBOW MAGIC is a trademark of Rainbow Magic Limited.
Reg. U.S. Patent & Trademark Office and other countries.
HIT and the HIT logo are trademarks of HIT Entertainment Limited.

12 11 10 9 8 7 6 5 4 3   11 12 13 14 15/0

Printed in the U.S.A.   40

First Scholastic Printing, July 2010

Phoebe
the Fashion Fairy

by Daisy Meadows

LITTLE APPLE

SCHOLASTIC INC.

New York   Toronto   London   Auckland
Sydney   Mexico City   New Delhi   Hong Kong

The Fairyland Palace

Clearing

The Village Hall

Twisty Lane

Wetherbury Village

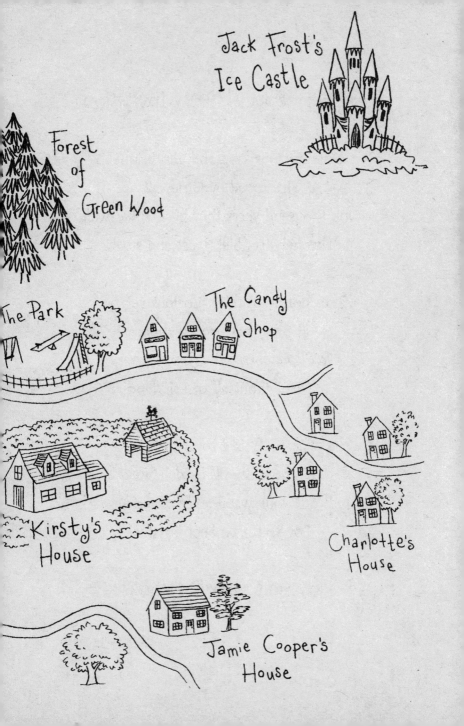

A Very Special Party Invitation

Our gracious king and gentle queen
Are loved by fairies all.
One thousand years they have ruled well,
Through troubles great and small.

In honor of their glorious reign
A party has been planned.
We'll celebrate their anniversary
Throughout all of Fairyland.

The party is a royal surprise,
We hope they'll be delighted.
So pull out your wand and fanciest dress . . .
For you have been invited!

RSVP: THE FAIRY GODMOTHER

Contents

Birthday Trouble

Kirsty Tate and Rachel Walker were busy wrapping a birthday present for Kirsty's friend, Charlotte.

"There," said Kirsty, tying the ribbon. "Charlotte's going to love this silver headband. It's so pretty!"

"Are you almost ready, girls?" Mrs. Tate called up the stairs. "Dad and I have to leave in two minutes!"

"We're coming, Mom," Kirsty replied.
Then she turned to Rachel. "I can't
believe we're going to another party, can
you?" She grinned.

Rachel shook her
head. "I wonder
what's going to
happen this time,"
she said excitedly.

The two girls
shared a secret.
They were friends
with the fairies!

And while Rachel had been staying
with Kirsty's family, the girls had been
helping the Party Fairies. Jack Frost
had sent his goblins into the human

world to cause trouble at parties. When a Party Fairy arrived to set things straight, a goblin would try to steal her magic party bag and take it back to Jack Frost! Rachel and Kirsty had been helping the fairies keep their party bags safe — so all the parties that week had been especially exciting.

Kirsty and Rachel put their party dresses into a bag with Charlotte's present, then rushed downstairs.

Kirsty's parents had to go out that afternoon, so Mrs. Tate had arranged for the girls to go to Charlotte's house a little early.

"We've helped almost all of the Party Fairies now," Kirsty said, as she and

Rachel walked along the road.

Rachel counted them off on her fingers. "Cherry the Cake Fairy, Melodie the Music Fairy, Grace the Glitter Fairy, Honey the Candy Fairy, and Polly the Party Fun Fairy," she said. "So the only two we haven't helped are . . ."

"Phoebe the Fashion Fairy and Jasmine the Present Fairy," Kirsty finished. "I wonder if we'll see one of them today."

Rachel couldn't help smiling as they walked up Charlotte's front path. "I bet we will," she said. "Those goblins won't be able to resist another chance to try to steal a magic party bag. One of them is bound to cause trouble! Then Phoebe or Jasmine will have to come and fix everything."

The girls knew that Jack Frost had sent his goblins to steal the party bags because he wanted to use fairy magic at a party of his own. He wanted his party to be better than the fairy king and queen's surprise anniversary party, which had been planned by the Fairy

Godmother to take place at the end
of the week. Kirsty and Rachel had
both been invited to the anniversary
celebration as special guests. They were
determined to make sure that Jack Frost
and his goblins didn't ruin everything by
stealing the Party Fairies' magic.

Kirsty rang the doorbell. A few
moments later, Charlotte answered
the door.

"Happy birthday!"
cried Kirsty and
Rachel together.

But then Kirsty
noticed how sad
her friend looked.
"Is everything all
right?" she asked,
concerned.

Charlotte didn't seem to be in a birthday mood. She wasn't wearing a party dress, and she wasn't even smiling. "No," she wailed. "Everything is *not* all right. My favorite dress is ruined!"

"Ruined?" Rachel echoed. "What happened?"

Charlotte held the front door open. "Come upstairs and see," she said miserably.

Kirsty and Rachel gasped when they saw Charlotte's white-and-gold party dress hanging on the door of her closet. It had messy splotches of what looked like green paint all over it.

"Oh, no!" Kirsty gasped. "How did that happen?"

Charlotte looked close to tears.

"I don't know," she said. "This

morning, it was totally clean!"

Charlotte's mom, Mrs. Ingle, came in. Her mouth fell open when she saw Charlotte's stained dress. "Charlotte!" she exclaimed. "You haven't been painting in your best dress, have you?"

"No," Charlotte cried. "I just came upstairs and found it like this!"

Mrs. Ingle frowned. "I hope your brother didn't have anything to do with it," she said, marching over to open the window. "Will!" she called down to the yard. "Come here!"

Charlotte's little brother, Will, scampered into the bedroom a few minutes later. He was covered in mud and looked very pleased with himself. "I found tons of worms," he told the girls happily, holding up a small muddy shovel.

"Will, your sister's party is starting soon." Mrs. Ingle groaned. "You were supposed to be getting ready."

Will glanced over at Charlotte. "Well, Charlotte isn't ready yet—and it's her party!" he protested.

"Speaking of which," Mrs. Ingle went on, "do you know anything about this?"

She showed Will Charlotte's party dress,

and he shook his head. "I've been outside all morning!" he insisted.

Charlotte nodded. "It's true, Mom," she said. "I saw him."

Mrs. Ingle sighed. "Well, I guess the dress must have brushed against something," she said, looking confused.

Rachel and Kirsty glanced around the room uneasily. They were both wondering if the dress really had brushed against something — or if somebody had ruined it on purpose.

Both girls knew it was just the kind of thing a goblin would do! And the green paint on the dress was an unmistakable goblin green.

Rachel caught Kirsty's eye and realized that they were both thinking the same thing — a goblin must be hiding somewhere very close by!

Hide-and-seek

Mrs. Ingle looked at her watch. "We have one hour before the party starts," she said. "We could run over to the dry cleaner's and see if they can help, but I still have to frost the cupcakes. I don't know how I'll get everything done in time." She frowned.

"We can decorate the cupcakes while you're out," Kirsty suggested cheerfully.

"Yes," Rachel added. "We're good at it," she said, remembering the icing they'd made at Kirsty's birthday party.

Mrs. Ingle smiled. "That's very nice of you, girls," she said. "Are you sure you wouldn't mind?"

"Of course not. It will be fun," Kirsty replied at once.

Mrs. Ingle led the girls downstairs. Mr. Ingle took Will away to get him cleaned up, and Mrs. Ingle took Rachel and Kirsty into the dining room. The party food was all set out on the table: one tray of cupcakes, one bowl of icing, a piping bag for squeezing the icing in pretty designs, and some cake decorations.

"This is really helpful, girls," Mrs. Ingle said. "Thank you!"

Then Charlotte and her mom hurried off to the dry cleaner's with

Charlotte's ruined dress.

As soon as Kirsty
and Rachel heard
Mrs. Ingle's car
leave the
driveway, they
looked at each
other meaningfully.

"We've got to find
that goblin," Kirsty said in
a low voice, "before he does
anything else to ruin the party."

"Well, he must have been in
Charlotte's bedroom recently. Let's
go back up and see if he's still there,"
Rachel suggested.

The girls made their way upstairs to
Charlotte's room. Kirsty put her finger to

her lips, then crept up to the closet and opened the doors wide.

Rachel's heart was pounding as she and Kirsty peeked inside. Jack Frost's goblins were very sneaky. You could never tell where they were going to pop up!

But there was no sign of the goblin in Charlotte's closet, so Kirsty searched under the bed while Rachel checked behind the curtains.

Then Rachel looked under Charlotte's bedspread and Kirsty checked on all of the shelves.

"Either he's hiding somewhere really, really sneaky, or he left the room," Kirsty said at last.

Rachel sighed. "He could be anywhere in the house by now," she said, "just waiting to cause more trouble!"

Kirsty glanced at her watch. "Come on, we'd better start those cupcakes," she said. "Otherwise *we'll* be the ones ruining Charlotte's party!"

Downstairs, Kirsty and Rachel began frosting the cupcakes, trying to think where the goblin might be hiding. Kirsty piped icing onto each cake, while Rachel decorated them with sprinkles.

Rachel was just finishing the last cupcake when Kirsty nudged her. "Look!" she cried.

Rachel looked up just in time to see

a stream of tiny, sparkly, red hearts
floating past the window.

Both girls ran over to take a closer
look. They couldn't believe their eyes!
There, waving at them through the
glass, was a beautiful, smiling fairy!

Goblin Attack

"It's Phoebe the Fashion Fairy!"
Rachel cried, opening the window for
her.

Phoebe had wavy blond hair, held
back by a wide crimson headband.
She wore a little white dress with a
row of red hearts around the hem, and
matching shoes. Her scarlet wand let

off ruby hearts that glittered in the
sunlight.

She fluttered inside and perched on the
windowsill. "Hello!" she said in a bright,
silvery voice. "Kirsty and Rachel, right?
I remember seeing you when Honey the
Candy Fairy showed you around the
Party Fairy workshop."

"That's right," Kirsty said. "And I remember your gorgeous fashion department, with all those wonderful, sparkly fairy dresses."

Phoebe nodded and then looked serious. "Now, I heard that there was a party dress disaster here, so I've come to work a little bit of fairy magic and fix everything."

"Well, we're very glad to see you," Kirsty said. She quickly filled Phoebe in on what had happened to Charlotte's special dress.

Phoebe's delicate features creased into a frown. "That does sound like goblin mischief," she agreed. "We'll have to be careful."

"We'll just clean up the decorating supplies," Rachel said, "and then we'll show you where Charlotte's bedroom is."

Kirsty arranged the cupcakes on a

plate while Rachel started gathering the icing equipment. Phoebe fluttered over for a closer look at the cupcakes. "Cherry the Cake Fairy would be proud of you two," she said, hovering over the table. "These look good enough for the king and queen of Fairyland!"

Rachel was frowning. "Where's the

icing bag?" she asked Kirsty. "I don't see it anywhere."

Kirsty looked around. "It was there a minute ago," she said, pointing to one end of the table.

"I know," Rachel agreed, sounding puzzled. "But it's gone."

No sooner had she said that than the lid of Will's nearby toy box flew open with a loud crash. The girls and Phoebe spun around to see a goblin bursting out of the box like a grinning, green jack-in-the-box.

"It's the goblin!" Kirsty cried.

"With the icing bag!" Rachel added.

The goblin held up the icing bag and squeezed it hard. A jet of icing shot out and hit Phoebe right in the stomach!

"Help!" she cried in surprise, tumbling backward.

Kirsty and Rachel watched in horror as Phoebe fell through the air. Luckily, she landed in the big, soft, strawberry Jell-O mold in the middle of the table and bounced up into the air again. Her arms flailed as she tried to recover her balance.

SQUISH! Phoebe plunged back into the Jell-O. She wasn't hurt, but this time she lost hold of her magic party bag. It flew across the table.

"Just what I was looking for," the goblin cackled, leaping out of the toy box.

Rachel gasped. "Oh, no you don't!" she cried, dashing around the table to try to reach the party bag before the goblin could take it.

But she was too late. The goblin's green hand closed around Phoebe's shimmering party bag, seconds before Rachel could get to it.

Nobody Home

The goblin gave a nasty grin, snatched
a cupcake in his other hand, and leaped
out of the window into the backyard.

"Oh, no!" Phoebe gasped, struggling
out of the sticky Jell-O. "I need my party
bag, or I won't be able to fix Charlotte's
dress!"

"And we all know what the goblin will

do with it," Kirsty groaned. "He'll give it to Jack Frost for his party."

"We can't let that happen," Phoebe said firmly, brushing chunks of red Jell-O from her dress. She waved her wand. Sparkling red hearts streamed from the tip and spilled all over Kirsty and Rachel. "I'll make you fairy-size," she said. "Then we can all fly after the goblin."

Kirsty and Rachel shut their eyes as Phoebe's magic started working. They felt themselves shrinking! Beautiful, shimmering fairy wings appeared on their backs, and Rachel couldn't resist doing a little flip. Being able to fly was so much fun!

Phoebe fluttered out the window, and the girls followed. They could see the goblin racing through the yard, greedily stuffing the cupcake into his mouth as he ran.

He glanced over his shoulder and spotted the three fairies zooming after

him. A look of panic crossed his face and he glanced around wildly, searching for somewhere to hide. The next moment he spotted the playhouse at the far end of the yard. He charged toward it, diving inside and slamming the door.

Phoebe was the first to reach the playhouse. She knocked loudly on the door. "Let me in!" she ordered.

"There's nobody home!" called the goblin from inside.

Phoebe tried to pull the door open, but the goblin must have been holding onto the handle on the other side, because it didn't move.

"It's no use, I'm not strong enough," Phoebe said, sighing.

"If you turn us back into girls, we might

be able to do it," Kirsty suggested.

"Good idea," Phoebe said, waving her wand again to release another stream of red hearts.

Kirsty and Rachel felt their arms and legs tingling with fairy magic as they grew back to their normal size.

"Okay!" Rachel said, grabbing the door handle. "Let's get this door open."

There was a scraping sound from inside the playhouse. Then, to Rachel's dismay, she found that she couldn't even turn the handle. "The goblin must have wedged something under the door handle," she cried in frustration. "A chair or something—it won't turn at all now!"

Phoebe groaned. "What are we going to do?" she asked anxiously.

Kirsty looked around, desperately
trying to think. Seeing the cake crumbs
that the goblin had dropped on the grass
gave her an idea. Obviously, the goblin
liked the cupcakes she and Rachel had
decorated . . . maybe they could tempt

him out with some more.
She whispered her idea
to Phoebe and Rachel,
and they both nodded
approvingly.
"Goblins always
want to get their
hands on more treats."
Phoebe laughed. "It's a great idea!" She
turned back toward the Ingles' house
and waved her wand with an expert
twirl.

Kirsty and Rachel watched in delight
as a stream of twinkling red hearts
shot straight from Phoebe's
wand into Charlotte's
house. A moment
later, something
very strange
happened. . . .

"Are those what I
think they are?" Kirsty
asked, staring.

"Flying cupcakes!" Rachel gasped.

A small procession of cupcakes was
zooming through the air toward the
playhouse in a neat "V" formation.

Kirsty's spirits rose as she saw the
goblin peeking curiously out of one of
the playhouse windows. He licked his

lips when he saw the flying cupcakes.

"He sees them!" Phoebe whispered to the girls, crossing her fingers.

The cupcakes landed neatly on the playhouse windowsill and started dancing  around, right under the goblin's nose.

"He looks tempted," Rachel said hopefully.

The goblin had his face eagerly pressed up against the glass, but then he caught sight of the girls looking at him. A determined expression came over his face. "If you think I'm coming out for a few tiny cupcakes, you've got another thing coming!" he yelled, folding his arms stubbornly. "I know it's a trick, and I'm staying here!"

Rachel sighed. She'd been sure the greedy goblin wouldn't be able to resist more cupcakes. Then she glanced down at her watch and gulped. "Oh, no! We've only got ten minutes before Charlotte's party starts," she cried.

Kirsty looked at her with wide eyes. "Charlotte and her mom will be back any second!" she exclaimed. "We've got to get that goblin out, right now!"

A Wave of Inspiration

Kirsty, Rachel, and Phoebe looked around the yard, wondering what to try next. When Rachel spotted the garden hose, her eyes lit up as a thought popped into her head. "How about this?" she asked the other two. "We put the end of the hose down the chimney, turn the water on, and flood the goblin out of the playhouse!"

Kirsty giggled. "I love it!" she said.

Phoebe was smiling, too. "Goblins don't like water, and they *hate* getting cold, wet feet," she added. "If anything's going to get him out of there, a cold shower will."

Quickly, Kirsty dangled the end of the hose down the playhouse chimney,

while Rachel ran to turn on the outside
faucet. A few seconds later, there was a
huge *SPLASH!*—quickly followed by a
surprised scream from the goblin.

"Where's that rain coming from?" he
grumbled. "I'm getting wet."

"Then come out," Phoebe called. "It's
nice and dry out here!"

More water splashed into the playhouse, and the goblin's moans grew louder. "Now my feet are wet," he groaned. "Ugh, horrible cold water. Make it stop!"

"We'll make it stop, if you come out and give Phoebe her party bag," Kirsty offered.

"No way!" the goblin answered rudely. "This party bag is mine now, and I'm going to give it to Jack Frost!"

"Well, you can't say we didn't warn you," Rachel shouted, turning the faucet on all the way. "Here comes the flood!"

Water poured into the playhouse.
Through the window, the girls and
Phoebe could see the goblin bobbing
around helplessly as the water level rose.

Then he floated against the small chair
he'd used to keep the door shut. He
accidentally kicked the chair aside, and
the playhouse door flew open.

"Help!" cried the goblin, as a huge wave of water gushed out of the door, carrying him along on top of it.

"I didn't know goblins could surf!" Rachel laughed as he sailed past her. She stretched out an arm and snatched Phoebe's party bag from his hands. "Got it!" she declared happily, passing the bag to Phoebe.

The goblin shrieked and flopped around in the river of water, trying to get to his feet. But it was impossible. The rushing stream carried him all the way down the backyard to the Ingles' koi pond. *SPLASH!* The goblin spilled right into the pond.

Kirsty, Rachel, and Phoebe couldn't help giggling as they watched the goblin

climb out, dripping wet and with a huge clump of weeds stuck to his head. He looked very glum.

"I'm almost tempted to twirl my wand to give him a special outfit," Phoebe laughed. "A swimsuit, goggles, and a nice, flowery swim cap!"

SQUISH, SQUISH, SQUISH!

The goblin stomped away, defeated.

"I think that's the last we'll see of our soggy friend today," Kirsty said with a grin.

Rachel ran to turn the water off, and then waved frantically at Phoebe and Kirsty. "Mrs. Ingle's back with Charlotte!" she yelled. "I just heard the car!"

Kirsty's face fell. Not only was the whole backyard a mud pit now, but the playhouse was a mess, the big, red Jell-O mold was ruined, and she and Rachel were all wet, too! How were they going to explain everything to Mrs. Ingle?

"Leave it to me," Phoebe said quickly. "You keep Charlotte's mom talking. I'll fix the playhouse first and then the dining room. Now, hurry!"

Kirsty and Rachel ran into the house to find poor Charlotte looking more upset than ever. "The cleaners said they'd never seen anything like this paint," she explained sadly. "They tried all kinds of things to get it off my dress, but nothing worked."

Mrs. Ingle put a comforting arm around her daughter. "Never mind," she said. "You've got lots of other nice things to wear. I know that dress is special to you, but you'll just have to choose

something else." She glanced over at Kirsty and Rachel as Charlotte began to trudge upstairs. "And you two should change, too," Mrs. Ingle added. "The party's going to start any minute." A frown appeared on her face as she noticed Rachel and Kirsty's wet clothes. "You look soaked. Are you all right?" she asked.

"Um . . ." Kirsty began, not sure how to explain.

"We're fine," Rachel said quickly. "We just got a little wet when we were washing up the things for the icing, that's all."

Mrs. Ingle's frown lifted. "I'd completely

forgotten about the cupcakes," she said.
"Did you get them all decorated?" She
walked toward the dining room door.

"Well, um, we . . ." Rachel mumbled,
crossing her fingers as she followed Mrs.
Ingle into the room.

Could Phoebe possibly have had time to magically clean up the playhouse *and* fix everything in the dining room? Rachel and Kirsty weren't sure . . . but they were about to find out, ready or not!

A Dress to Impress

Kirsty and Rachel should not have worried. Phoebe had worked wonders! The cupcakes were neatly arranged on their plate, and the Jell-O was its perfect wobbly self again. Nobody could even imagine that a Party Fairy had fallen into it just twenty minutes earlier!

Kirsty blinked as she noticed a tiny glimmer of sparkly red light flicker around the table, then vanish quickly. She turned to Rachel, and Rachel nodded. She had seen it, too. One last sparkle of fairy magic!

Luckily, Mrs. Ingle had not noticed anything—she was too busy admiring the cupcakes. "You're talented, girls," she said. "I couldn't have decorated them more beautifully myself—thank you so much!"

"You're welcome," Kirsty said, smiling with relief. "Now, we'd better go and get changed."

Just then, there was an excited cry from upstairs. "Kirsty, Rachel! Come here . . . now!"

Kirsty and Rachel rushed up to Charlotte's room. To their amazement, hanging on the closet door were three beautiful party dresses. One was a deep red, covered in golden hearts, with a matching headband. A tag hanging from the sleeve said CHARLOTTE in pretty, sparkly writing.

The other two dresses had tags that read KIRSTY and RACHEL. Kirsty's dress was pink with a lilac dragonfly embroidered near the hem, and Rachel's dress was purple with pink butterflies around the neckline.

"This is the most beautiful dress ever," Charlotte whispered, stroking the shimmering red material. "But where did it come from?"

Rachel opened her mouth, but couldn't think of a single thing to say. How could they explain that the three outfits were fairy gifts, created by Phoebe the Fashion Fairy?

"Happy birthday, Charlotte!" Kirsty cried, thinking quickly. "It's our present to you. We, um, went and got it while you were out—just in case the cleaners couldn't fix your dress."

"And here's a little something else, too,"
Rachel added, pulling the present they'd
wrapped earlier out of the bag. "Happy
birthday!"

"Oh, thank you!"
Charlotte cried happily,
hugging both girls.

As Charlotte started
opening the present,
Kirsty suddenly nudged
Rachel.

Rachel turned to see what her friend
had spotted. To her delight, the dragonfly
and butterflies on their party dresses were
fluttering their delicate embroidered
wings and sparkling with golden lights.
She grinned at Kirsty—they were both
going to be wearing magic dresses!

Charlotte was pulling off the last piece

of wrapping paper. "What a pretty
necklace!" she exclaimed, holding it up.
"I love it."

Kirsty and Rachel stared. The silver
headband they'd wrapped for
Charlotte back at Kirsty's
house had been turned
into a golden necklace
with three, heart-
shaped red beads strung
in the middle.

Phoebe's work again, I bet, Kirsty thought,
smiling.

Charlotte pulled on her dress and
Rachel fastened the necklace around her
neck.

"I have to go and show Mom,"
Charlotte said, twirling around happily.

"Thank you so much. This is turning out to be the best birthday I've ever had!"

As soon as Charlotte had left the room, Phoebe peeked out from behind a curtain. With a smile, she waved her wand. Kirsty and Rachel suddenly found themselves wearing their new party dresses! Their old clothes were neatly folded in piles on the bed.

"Oh, Phoebe, these dresses are just gorgeous," Kirsty declared, standing in front of the mirror. "Thank you!"

"I feel like a fairy all over again, wearing this," Rachel added, dancing around in her new dress.

Phoebe's cheeks blushed pink. "Oh, it's nothing," she said, looking incredibly happy. "I'm just doing my job. Glad to help!" Then she smiled. "Anyway, I should be thanking *you* for saving my party bag from the goblin."

"Oh, it's nothing." Kirsty grinned.

"We're glad to help, too." Rachel laughed.

"Just doing our job!" they chorused together.

Phoebe came over and hugged them both.

"Have a wonderful party," she said. "I have to fly back to Fairyland now."

Kirsty and Rachel waved good-bye as Phoebe disappeared in a swirl of glittering fairy dust.

Then the doorbell rang downstairs. "Charlotte's friends are here," Kirsty said with a grin. "Let's go and have some fun. I think we've earned it today."

"We definitely have," Rachel agreed. "I can't wait for our next adventure!"

THE PARTY FAIRIES

Cherry, Melodie, Grace,
Honey, Polly, and Phoebe
all have their magic party bags
back. Now Rachel and Kirsty
need to help the last Party Fairy,

Jasmine
the Present Fairy!

Join their next adventure
in this special sneak peek. . . .

"Look at all those booths, Rachel,"
Kirsty Tate said, pointing down the street
where she lived. "This is going to be
a great party!"

All of Kirsty's neighbors were rushing
around setting up booths and tables
outside their houses. There were all
kinds of things going on, from games

and raffles to booths selling homemade jams and cakes. Delicious smells wafted toward the girls from the barbecue at the other end of the street. The road was closed to traffic, and people were already milling around in the sunshine, enjoying the fair.

"I think having a street party is a great idea," Rachel Walker, Kirsty's best friend, said with a grin. "I wish we had one on our street back home." Rachel had come to stay with Kirsty for the week of school break.

Kirsty was opening the last box of books. "We'd better hurry and put these on the table," she said. "Lots of people are showing up now."

"I'm glad the block party is today, before I go home tomorrow," Rachel said, helping Kirsty arrange the books around the booth that Mr. and Mrs. Tate were running. "I hope we raise lots of money for charity."

"We always do," said Kirsty happily, neatly stacking the books. "People come to the party from all over town. But"—she lowered her voice—"we'll have to be extra-careful this year, won't we?"

Rachel nodded seriously. "Yes," she agreed. "A party means we have to keep our eyes out for goblin mischief!"

"I'm not going to let Jack Frost's goblins ruin our block party," Kirsty said in a determined voice. "Or the king and queen's celebration!"

RAINBOW magic™

There's Magic in Every Series!

The Rainbow Fairies
The Weather Fairies
The Jewel Fairies
The Pet Fairies
The Fun Day Fairies
The Petal Fairies
The Dance Fairies
The Music Fairies
The Sports Fairies
The Party Fairies

Read them all!

■ SCHOLASTIC

www.scholastic.com
www.rainbowmagiconline.com

SCHOLASTIC and associated
logos are trademarks and/or
registered trademarks of Scholastic Inc.
©2010 Rainbow Magic Limited.
HIT and the HIT Entertainment logo are
trademarks of HIT Entertainment Limited.

HiT entertainment

RMFAIRY2

RAINBOW magic™

SPECIAL EDITION

Three Books in One—
More Rainbow Magic Fun!

HIT and the HIT Entertainment logo are
trademarks of HIT Entertainment Limited.
© 2010 Rainbow Magic Limited.
SCHOLASTIC and associated logos are trademarks
and/or registered trademarks of Scholastic Inc.

■■SCHOLASTIC
www.scholastic.com
www.rainbowmagiconline.com

HiT entertainment

RMSPECIAL3

RAINBOW magic

These activities are magical!
Play dress-up, send friendship notes, and much more!

HIT and the HIT Entertainment logo are
trademarks of HIT Entertainment Limited.
© 2010 Rainbow Magic Limited.
SCHOLASTIC and associated logos are trademarks
and/or registered trademarks of Scholastic Inc.

■SCHOLASTIC

www.scholastic.com
www.rainbowmagiconline.com

HIT entertainment

RMACTIV3